T0157348

Like the Melody that's *Sweetly* Played in Tune

Like the Melody that's *Sweetly* Played in Tune[1]

Tom Grifa

Illustrations by Gary Bartholomew

Illustrations by Gary Bartholomew

Archway Publishing books may be ordered through booksellers or by contacting:

Archway Publishing
1663 Liberty Drive
Bloomington, IN 47403
www.archwaypublishing.com
1 (888) 242-5904

ISBN: 978-1-4808-3150-6 (sc)
ISBN: 978-1-4808-3151-3 (e)

Library of Congress Control Number: 2016907677

Print information available on the last page.

Archway Publishing rev. date: 6/14/2016

CONTENTS

Dedication vii
Foreword ix

Chapter 1: "A Midsummer Night's Dream"? 1
Chapter 2: Liga From Latvia 9
Chapter 3: The Merchant of Ecinev 13
Chapter 4: Two Gentlemen From Anorev 20
Chapter 5: The Taming of the Shrew Mouse 25
Chapter 6: The Comedy of Errors 30
Chapter 7: Measure for Measure 34
Chapter 8: Much Ado About Nothing 39
Chapter 9: All's Well … (So Far!) 44
Chapter 10: The Third Richard III 50
Chapter 11: A Winter's Tale 55
Chapter 12: All's Well That Ends Well 61
Chapter 13: Epilogue 65

Endnotes 67

DEDICATION

TO MY GOOD FRIEND MEL, WHO, AT AGE 8, IS ALREADY ONE OF THE BRIGHTEST STARS IN OUR WORLD.

YOU ARE THE INSPIRATION FOR THIS WORK, JUST AS YOU HAVE BEEN AN INSPIRATION TO ALL OF US WHO KNOW AND LOVE YOU.

IT IS MY HOPE THAT I HAVE IN SOME SMALL WAY CAPTURED YOUR SPIRIT ON THESE PAGES.

FOREWORD

BY JUDY GRIFA

LIKE THE MELODY THAT'S SWEETLY PLAYED IN TUNE, which you are about to read, is a wondrous tale that describes a journey which we all take in life to find our destiny. The journey is imaginative, filled with literary allusions to great literature, and inspirational in its advice to all who read it.

Tom Grifa's inspiration for this story is also pretty extraordinary. The main character, Meladie, is modeled after a very precocious eight year old whose intelligence and demeanor can also be found in the book's main character, an extremely bright, curious, and talented eight year old, wise beyond her years. Her imagination, courage, and creativity are what inspired Tom to write about this journey through the maze of life.

The reader is truly in for a treat. What a joy to read!

CHAPTER I

"A Midsummer Night's Dream"?

Meladie's awakening in the middle of the night was something she rarely ever did. She usually slept so soundly. And although she was an early riser, she had never arisen this early, for It was just after midnight. When she opened her eyes, the third story room where she slept with her sister for some reason seemed to be as bright as midday. She looked to the twin bed where her older sister Madison was sound asleep with a quiet snore that was little more than heavy breathing. The light of the full moon pierced the room through the curtained windows, making everything visible as though it were noon.

When she sat up, she saw what had never been there before. Right smack in the middle of the outside wall between the two curtained windows was a pink door. "How could that be?" she wondered in a quiet whisper. It had never been there before to her knowledge. She was certain she would have noticed.

The thought occurred to her that she might not be awake at all, but just dreaming. How could she know? She thought of Dickens' "Bah Humbug" character who mistrusted his ghosts because he thought that he might have been dreaming, but she quickly dismissed the dream possibility with her conclusion that it did not really matter. It was very astute of her to conclude that dreams are really the same as being awake. We experience them just as we do reality. So as not to waken her older sister, Meladie quietly slipped from her bed to approach the pink door. Her curiosity would not allow her to do otherwise, for what if she fell back to sleep only to find that the door was not there when she awoke in the morning?

As she crept up to the door, she noticed a small sign with an arrow pointing toward the door knob. "OPEN HERE" it directed.

"What a silly sign," she mused. "Anyone would know that a doorknob would be used to open the door." But her random thought quickly turned suspicious when she considered that her bedroom happened to be on the third floor of their home. What if she opened the door and was sucked out by the wind to fall past her parents' bedroom on the second floor and past the kitchen on the first only to land in the rock garden below, for she knew there had never been a stairway on that side of the house.

She did not know what to do. If only Madison were awake she could ask her advice. She stepped quietly to the side of Madison's bed and gave her a shake.

"Maddie," she said in a whispered shout. Without opening her eyes Madison plainted "Oh leave me alone and let me sleep." She rolled over, turning her back toward Meladie. Obviously, the option of getting Maddie's advice was not open to her. She would have to fend for herself. By nature, Meladie was a very logical thinker, knowing that if she should err, she should always err on the side of "low risk." But her alter-ego was very adventurous as well, and it was that side of her nature that pushed her forward to reach for the door knob.

She placed her hand on the knob without turning it, but immediately jumped back, for the door knob appeared to send a vibration of some sort up her arm and through her entire body. It was almost like a mild electrical shock which she understood much later to be what many called the "thrill of adventure" that came with experiencing something new. Not that opening a door was new to her, for she was eight years old and had already opened more than her share of doors.

She decided that perhaps she should consider this whole situation in greater depth before making the decision to move ahead. It was obvious that the side of "logic" was pulling her away. Meladie thought that she would get back in bed and close her eyes for awhile to see if the door would still be there when she opened them again.

As she moved away from the door toward her bed, she caught a glimpse of her pillow, on which rested another sign which simply stated, "FEAR NOT - GO BACK!"

"Now what is to be made of that?" she queried. After all, Meladie prided herself in doing whatever was necessary, regardless of any trepidations she might have. She had little patience with those who could not do the same.

Her mind was made up. Once decided, she could 'brave' herself through anything. Which is exactly what she did.

She approached the pink door once again, resolved to absorb that initial "thrill of adventure," and reached for the knob once more. But this time, there was nothing. There was not the slightest bit of any vibration whatsoever. Had she just imagined it before?

As unsettling as the situation was (for Meladie was not pleased when she could not come up with 'reasons' for any given situation), she resolved to try the door. A slight twist to the right and a gentle pull was all she needed. The door opened. Meladie immediately felt a cooling breeze on her face and in her hair. And then she saw! It was the most amazing sight she could have imagined. She could see far beyond the tops of the trees which served as the citadel of their family estate. She saw the snow-covered mountains far in the distance enwrapped by the azure sky and billowing white clouds.

The view was simply magnificent. It seemed to cry out to her that she should follow the pathway which was suspended in mid-air from the doorway to far beyond her ken. Meladie stood in wonder at the sight of it all, and, adventurous as she was, it did not take her long to make the first step onto the pathway, for her curiosity would not be subdued. While stepping gingerly at first, for there were no railings to safeguard her steps, she was soon moving forth with reckless abandon, determined to find where this magical path would take her. She crossed over the open space beneath her and was walking among the treetops which at first were just slightly above her head. As the pathway very gradually descended, she could no longer see the mountains in the distance. She paused a moment to catch her breath and looked back. It was then that she realized that the pathway behind her was gone. It was disappearing with each step she took. She knew at this point there was no turning back.

She calculated having walked at least a kilometer or perhaps a mile, she was not sure which. She never did really understand why everyone made such a fuss over calling them one or the other. The highway signs that had both only served to confuse the issue and provoke arguments among adults who thought one system was better than the other. More importantly, she calculated that the pathway had dropped in altitude approximately one story; therefore, if her bedroom were 3 stories high and each story were 10 feet high, (3 x 10 = 30; 30 - 10 = 20) She was still approximately 20 feet up in the trees. If her descent continued at the same pace, then she would reach solid ground in 2 "kilo-miles." (She knew there was no such measurement, but it suited her purposes and she did not have to argue about which system should be used.)

Having been so absorbed in her calculations, she hadn't realized that she had come almost face-to-face with a creature whose slight movement caught her eye. She was a bit startled until she recognized the being to be an owl who appeared to be more startled than she.

"Who are you?" she asked.

"Whoo am I?" queried the owl. "I already know whoo I am, so you must tell me whoo yoo are."

"I'm Meladie."

"Well, if yooooo are not going to tell me the truth, there is no point in our speaking to one another. I am on to yooo. Yoooo cannot be melody," declared the owl.

"No, it's true. I'm Meladie. That's my name."

"Impossible!" the owl stated very firmly. "I know what a melody is. It's a term for a tune or song. A person cannot be a melody."

"But it's true. You see, my sister was a musician, and when I was born …" Meladie stopped in mid sentence, for she knew that the owl was looking askance and would not be willing to accept her explanation. "I guess owls are not always as 'wise' as they profess," she thought to herself.

"Why don't you just call me "Mel" for short and we need not bother about a tune or a song?" Meladie asked, hoping that her suggestion would solve the problem.

"Why Mel for short?" queried the owl. "Yooo are already twice as tall as I and still growing taller right before my eyes. I should call yooo by yooor full name, which must be Melvin."

"Really, owl?" she said rather disgustedly. "So what's your name?"

"Well now that we have been properly introduced, Melvin, I suppose that I should tell yoooo that my name is Puck. I come from a 'Midsummer Night's

Dream,' which you may or may not be having. The question is, 'Are you dreaming or not?'"

Meladie could not answer the question because she really did not know if she was dreaming. But a thought occurred to her about this owl's name.

"Well if Meladie cannot be a name," she suggested, "neither can Puck be a name!"

"What do yoooo mean by that, young lady?" asked the owl indignantly.

"Well, you see, a puck is just an object that hockey players bat about the ice; therefore it cannot be a name either," stated Meladie very emphatically.

"Oh! Yooo do make a good point," said the owl. He could see that this young lady was not one to be bullied. "Your power of reasoning is formidable. Very formidable!. I therefore concede the issue and proclaim that Melody can and shall be used as a name."

"Well thank you," said Meladie. "And I shall proclaim and concede that Puck may also be used as a name."

Having settled the name issue, Meladie went on to ask, ""Do you live up here in this tree?".

"Why do yooooo say 'Up here' when yoooo really mean 'down here?'"

"I say 'up here' because you are up in a tree!" exclaimed Meladie.

"But didn't yoooo come 'down here' to visit?" asked the owl.

"Why, yes, I came down to get here, but … must you be so precise? You make things very difficult, you know."

"Difficult, yoooo say! Oh, dear, oh dear. I must change my ways. I must or I will have my responsibilities taken from me," cried the owl. "Yoooo see, I have been charged with the responsibility of looking after yooooo. And I have been called upon to set yoooo on your way with a small token of something that may help yoooo in your travels."

With that, the owl reached under his right wing with his left (or was it his left wing with his right?) but looked seriously dismayed, for he found nothing. " Oooo my, oooo my! he exclaimed. I fear I've lost it."

"Perhaps you should look under your other wing," suggested Meladie.

"Oh, yes, yes. Of course," said he. "You are so perceptive. Right wing, left wing. I don't know what to think. All I know is I'm in the middle of it all."

With that, the owl pulled out a small draw string purse from under his other wing and handed it to Meladie. She took the bag and examined its contents, which appeared to be nothing more than a handful of sawdust of some sort.

"How can this possibly help me?" asked Meladie. "It's only sawdust, you know."

Putting the tip of his wing to his beak, the owl warned, "Shhh! Yoooo mustn't say that out loud. Others might hear yooo. And remember, my Dear, what might appear to have little value will, if packaged nicely, become more valuable to others. It's all in the packaging, my Dear."

Meladie looked once again at the draw-string bag and had to admit that it was nicely packaged for sawdust. "What should I do with it, Puck?"

"Too many questions! Too many questions!"

"Toooo many questions! Toooo many questions!" cried the owl. "Be off with you and don't turn back. If ever yoooo are troubled by anyone or any thing, just look in your string purse for help. There may be magic in it. Now be on your way. I shall be watching."

"Before I go, I should like to know whether or not this is all a dream. I should expect that a wise owl such as the likes of you would at least be able to answer that one question without equivocation. The question is, 'Am I dreaming?'"

"Ah, of course," said the owl. "I always knewwww that with yooo there would be a question, but, yoooo see, it really matters not whether your experiences occur while you are awake or while you are asleep. You see, they are experiences nonetheless. What is truly important is that we learn from our experiences and seek more of them so that we can continue to learn. Let it suffice to say that the answer to your question lies in whatever your destiny is determined to be. Now that is all I have to say on the subject."

Now Meladie was not particularly happy with the owl's answer, but it seemed so typical of the owl to be evasive. Nevertheless, she turned to go, realizing that she must get on with her journey.

As she turned and started off, she decided to look once more in her newly acquired bag of sawdust. "Perhaps there was some sort of magic there after all," she thought.

When she opened the bag again, she noticed a small folded paper that she hadn't seen before. It was the size of the notes that were found in the fortune cookies that she enjoyed so much when shared by all in her family whenever they went to her favorite Chinese restaurant. Some of the fortunes were so profound that she thought perhaps there was a clue to answer her question.

She unfolded the note and read the following:

> "WE ARE SUCH STUFF AS DREAMS ARE MADE ON;
> AND OUR LITTLE LIFE IS ROUNDED WITH A SLEEP."[2]

"I'm not sure what this means," she thought to herself, "but perhaps someone along the way will be able to explain it."

Meladie tucked the little bag in her small pocket and resolutely started off as Puck had instructed, wondering what her destiny would be.

CHAPTER 2

Liga From Latvia

Meladie quickened her pace to make up for time lost speaking to Puck, the owl. At this time she didn't know if he were helpful or not, but she assumed that she would see him again, especially since he said that he would be watching. It was a bit comforting to think of him as a protector. After all, the pathway, which continued to descend very gradually, was quite lonely at this point.

She once again calculated her distance from the start. (1 kilomile to the owl - plus 1 kilomile to her present location = 2 kilomiles from home). The farther she got from home, the lonelier she felt, especially since the shadows were lengthening as the sun lowered itself to the treetops.

As she passed a rather sharp curve in the pathway, she could see to its end where it touched the ground in an open area very lush with a reassuring green so pleasant to the eye. Meladie was not sure she had ever before seen such a beautiful sight as she scampered quickly to reach solid ground at last. Her final step off the pathway was more of a leap than a stride as both feet hit the ground simultaneously and, although she saw no one there, she experienced a feeling both of contentment and achievement in having come so far on her own.

Meladie took a long look back to where the pathway had been, but it was no longer there. It has disappeared completely into the darkening sky. She realized there was no turning back at this point; she turned resolutely to continue moving forward when she began to feel weary. It was time to sleep, but where? Certainly not in the open meadow, even though it was beautifully pleasant enough.

She scanned the entire outskirts of the meadow's fringe when something which she hadn't seen before caught her eye. As she moved toward it, she realized it to be a sizable stack of hay, a welcomed sight. Without hesitation, Meladie nestled into what was to be her bed for the night, every bit as comfortable as the one she left at home.

When she awakened the next morning, she fully expected to open her eyes to her own bedroom with Maddie still sound asleep in the bed next to hers; but that was not to be, for when she reached for her covers thinking that she could roll over for another lazy hour before getting out of bed, she sensed that she was not alone. With her eyes still shut and a cool but pleasant breeze to her face, she recalled the haystack where she had fallen asleep the night before.

Apprehensively, she forced her eyes to open only to see a face not more than 12 centa-inches from hers. The close proximity of another face caused her to sit straight up to a sitting position with a startled expression and a one word exclamation of "Oh!"

As Meladie's eyes came into focus, she saw before her a beautiful young girl of about 15 years with golden blond hair cropped tightly about her face. Meladie could not help but stare into her gorgeous icy blue eyes.

"Who are you?" she asked.

"Ah, You are avake finally. I am Liga from Latvia. Mr. Puck Owl send me to help you find your destiny."

"I am Liga from Latvia."

Meladie at once noticed that she had a foreign accent of some kind.

"You are very pretty and you have a lovely accent," said Meladie, hoping to make the young girl feel at ease. "I'm not exactly sure where Latvia is, but it must be a long way off."

"Oh yes, it is on other side of world near Russia. Three years ago, parents send me to Adanac because they think Russians are coming, and they want for me a better life, so I go to live with cousin."

"Adanac? I've never heard of Adanac. Is that in Michigan?"

"Oh no. It is large country north of Michigan."

"Do you mean Canada? Canada is the only country north of Michigan."

"Ah, Canada. Yes. That it. I get it always backwards. You see, my English not so good. But now I want go back to Latvia because Russians never come. Now it is safe for me, but I don't know way back. Mr. Puck Owl tell me if I assist you, you will help me too, yes?"

"I shall be glad to help you if I can, but you see I don't know where Latvia is, and I'm not quite sure where I am right now. It has all been so very confusing."

"Not to worry," said Liga reassuringly. "We find way together. Now is time to get out of haystack and begin. First I take you to get clothes so not to wear pajamas all day. We go to see Mr. Skylark, the merchant from Ecinev. He will sell you outfit to wear."

"But I have no money to buy an outfit!" exclaimed Meladie.

Once again Liga said, "Not to worry. You will make deal with him. He will drive hard bargain, but you can make agreement."

"Well I've never had to bargain before. Usually my family gets me everything I need," said Meladie. "This will certainly be a new adventure for me. The question is, will I know how to bargain?"

Liga simply smiled, knowing that Meladie would not only know how, but that she would do it well.

CHAPTER 3

The Merchant of Ecinev

Liga took Meladie by the hand and led her to the North side of the meadow. It could not have been more than a kilo-mile's walk, and the time passed quickly as Meladie enjoyed the beautiful wild flowers that filled the terrain with a blend of wonderful colors. The weather too was just perfect for a walk in such a pretty place.

As they approached the merchant's place of business, Meladie could see a very simple open stand which stood very near the edge of a cliff that overlooked the valley. The view was spectacular, but cause for some concern because the merchant behind the stand stood very close to the edge of the cliff.

Mr. Skylark, the merchant, was a rather slight man with a beak-like nose that made him look very like a bird.

"Bongiorno, signorinas!" he said.

"Hello," said Meladie. "At least I think that is what you said. But you see, I do not speak Italian."

"Ah, I see you are English. It is okay. We can do business in English," he said.

"But I'm not English. I am American," explained Meladie.

"Well then if you are American, why do you speak English?" questioned Mr. Skylark, the merchant. "Shouldn't you be speaking American?"

Liga could see that Meladie thought his question somewhat impertinent, so she quickly jumped in with, "Mr. Skylark, the English have loaned their language to the Americans while they make language of their own. It okay to do business in English."

"I see," said Mr. Skylark. "Why didn't you just say so in the first place," he said rudely.

Now Meladie did not like his manner at all. "Mr. Skylark, if you continue to be so rude, Liga and I will take our business elsewhere," she said resolutely. "I don't know why anyone would want to come here to do business.!"

"Well, you see," said Mr. Skylark, "they must come here because this is the only business this side of life's maze; so it doesn't seem to matter whether we treat our customers rudely or politely. It has no effect whatsoever on our sales."

"Well I would prefer to be treated politely if you don't mind," insisted Meladie with dignity and self pride.

Mr. Skylark could see that Meladie was not a pushover in any sense of any language so he backed down immediately. "I apologize if I have offended, and I shall treat you with every respect that a bona-fide customer deserves," he said, bowing his head slightly to one side.

Peacemaker Liga again jumped in with "That would be best for all." She could see that Meladie needed a second or two to calm herself.

Meladie did compose herself quickly, exhibiting a patience which she had rarely shown to those who did not seem to meet her standards. "We have come to purchase an outfit that would be suitable for my travels through 'life's maze,' as you put it. But I see that you have nothing to sell."

"Ah, but you are wrong to think that," cautioned Mr. Skylark. "Just tell me what you would like, and I shall show it to you as it will look when you wear it. Just step up to our mystical mirror and we shall be disposed to please you."

Meladie obliged by stepping up to the mirror, which seemed very ordinary to her.

Mr. Skylark went on, "Now tell me, have you ever seen someone wearing an outfit that you truly wished for yourself?"

"Well, not much comes to mind, although I thought the Michigan State University cheerleaders looked very beautiful in their green and white cheerleading outfits. And green is one of my favorite colors." said Meladie.

"Ah, a good beginning, said the merchant." On the side of the mirror, Mr. Skylark pushed a button called "input," and stated, "Green and white cheerleading outfit." He then hit a second button that was labeled "display," and, as he did so, Meladie's reflection was immediately transformed. She could now see that her pajamas were changed into the outfit she had described to the merchant. Meladie was not only amazed, but impressed as well that the mirror could do what it did. She looked down at herself and noticed that she was still wearing her pajamas, but her reflection showed that she was wearing the green and white outfit which the Michigan State University cheerleaders wore.

"My goodness!" she exclaimed. "That is truly amazing."

"My goodness!" she exclaimed. "That is truly amazing."

She liked the outfit very much. But upon reflection, her practical nature kicked in. "You know," she said to Liga, "I think this outfit is very nice, but not really suited for traveling through the meadow and the woods. Perhaps we should try something else," she said to the merchant.

He responded, "Can you think of another outfit that you have seen that you also like? Perhaps we can merge the two."

Meladie thought for a while, then added, "Well, when I read about Peter Pan, I thought the outfit he wore was very nice and practical too for his adventures. Does that help you at all?" she asked.

"Of course," said the merchant, confidently, as once again he pressed the input button and announced, "Merge the cheerleader with Peter Pan." As he hit the display button, once again Meladie's image changed in the mirror. Her image now showed her wearing a drab brown and green cheerleader's outfit.

"Oh, my!" she winced. "I think your mirror has it backwards. The color is wrong and so is the outfit. This won't do at all."

"Well then," said the merchant, "If it is backwards then you will need to face the other way, and we'll try again."

Now Meladie did not understand the merchant's reasoning, but she complied and turned her back to the mirror. She could hear the old Skylark pressing the input button once again and saying, "Now do it backwards." After hitting the display button, he told Meladie to turn and view the image.

Once again she complied and saw her image wearing the Pan-like outfit that was now a bright green and white.

"Why that's perfect," she declared. "I'll take it."

"Wonderful," said the merchant. "Now stand very still and we will finalize the sale. Remember, in the mirror, right is left and left is right. We must make it so we see ourselves the way we are seen by others.

Meladie knew that but raised her right hand to check, and sure enough it was her left hand raised in the mirror.

"Now be still, My Dear, and the transformation will be made."

He hit the input button for the last time, and chanted,

> "O, wad some Power the giftie gie us
> To see oursels as others see us!"[3]

This time old Skylark hit the "finalize sale" button. Meladie could feel a slight vibration of the scale, and she witnessed her image changing in the mirror. Her reflection now showed her wearing her pajamas while she now wore the outfit it had previously shown. The transformation was complete.

Liga stood looking at Meladie in total amazement. "Oh, Meladie, how wonderful you look! Your new outfit is just perfect for you."

Meladie too was pleased. Her harlequin tights in green and white would suit her purpose just fine. Of course she did not yet know exactly what her purpose was. She did know, however, that now she must bargain with Mr. Skylark for a good price. She was in a very difficult position, for she had no money.

"Now step over here to the counter to pay," said the Merchant. "That will be tuppence."

"I don't know what tuppence is. How much is that in American dollars?" she asked.

The merchant looked at Liga and said, "But you told me earlier that we could do business in English."

"But you see," said Liga, "I meant the language not the country," she insisted.

"Well then," exclaimed the merchant. "In American dollars the price will be much more. Let me see," he mused. "Hmm. That comes out to $463.79."

"Why that is outrageous!" shouted Meladie, not to be taken for a fool. "In America, we never pay that much for an outfit unless it is for a movie star who will only wear it once. I'll not pay that much."

"Ah, but if you are paying in American dollars you should be willing to pay much more because that is what American tourists do so they can take whatever they buy home to show their friends what it is that they bought in Venice," insisted the merchant.

Meladie thought that Mr. Skylark was driving a very hard bargain here. But Liga once again stepped in and pulled Meladie to the side to whisper, "Tell him that you will take it for tuppence. In England that is only two pennies. It is good bargain."

"Only two pennies," thought Meladie. "That is a good bargain."

She stepped back to the counter and looked the merchant directly in his eyes as she very firmly stated, "Mr. Skylark, I will bargain with you in English. I shall pay tuppence, but you see, I have no money."

Mr. Skylark looked at her very suspiciously and queried, "Then why do you carry that little sack with the pursestrings if you have no money?"

As Meladie reached for the pursestrings to explain, she said, "Oh, that is just my magic ..." She interrupted herself, for, when taking hold of the sack, she felt something hard and round. Reaching inside with her forefinger and thumb, she pulled out a coin which was labeled "tuppence."

She thought quickly, "Well, what I meant was I have no American money. I shall pay you tuppence and not a penny more."

The merchant thought carefully and offered, "Why then the price is tuppence and one ha'penny." He waited.

"But you said the price was tuppence," Meladie objected.

"But you said you would pay tuppence and not a penny more. A ha'penny is not a penny more. It is only a half penny more. So therefore I accept your latest offer of tuppence and a ha'penny," said the Merchant resolutely.

"But I only have tuppence!" insisted Meladie.

Once again the merchant looked at her suspiciously and glanced down at her purse. Meladie thought to check her purse again, and surely enough, there was another coin that magically appeared. As she lifted the coin from the purse, she saw that it was labeled "one ha'penny."

"A deal!" she exclaimed as she plunked the two coins down on the counter. "It was a pleasure doing business with you."

As she turned to Liga to leave, it was obvious that both the merchant and Meladie were quite happy with the bargain they had struck. Mr. Skylark was content with the fact that he managed to eke out a ha'penny more than he had first anticipated, and Meladie was happy to have reached an agreement knowing that her magic purse had saved the deal.

CHAPTER 4

Two Gentlemen From Anorev

It seemed to take Meladie and Liga a very long time to walk through this meadow pathway, which at times was very hilly and fraught with stones which made their journey somewhat uncomfortable. When Meladie complained that her feet hurt, Liga encouraged her to press on for it would not be much longer.

"Where are we going?" Meladie asked impatiently. She found this part of her adventure to be boring. It was her nature to get things over with quickly if they were not fun.

"You are too impatient," chided Liga. "You must keep focus for we will be there soon."

Meladie grew silent but plodded on, knowing Liga was right. Before long they approached a gradual hill which they had to ascend. Both were close to exhaustion by the time they reached the crest, where they could see what was beyond.

Meladie was awed by what she saw. Row after row of huge hedges were laid out before her, set in a maze of twists and turns and cul de sacs. It seemed to go on forever.

"What is this place?" she asked Liga.

"This is what they call the 'Maze of Life.' We must find our way through to reach our destiny."

Meladie was impressed. She was more than willing to take on what seemed to Liga to be an insurmountable undertaking.

"We can do this Liga. I know we can. C'mon. Let's get started."

"Wait!" said Liga, grabbing Meladie by the arm to hold her back. "We must move more like turtle and not like hare if we are to survive this journey and reach our destination. Once again I remind you not to be impatient."

Meladie knew that Liga was giving her good advice, but she remained anxious about moving along.

"First, we must meet up with two gentlemen at the entrance to maze," said Liga. "They will tell us how to get through maze. It is very difficult journey."

Meladie had no doubt that the journey would be difficult, but to her it was like one giant puzzle which she was certain that she could solve. Her critical thinking skills made her very good at puzzles.

After walking another one quarter kilo-mile, the two girls approached the maze where the two gentlemen from Anorev were busy setting out some Nailati cheeses near the end of a rope, which stretched into the maze and disappeared around a corner.

Noticing the two girls approaching, one gentleman said to the other, "Ah. We have guests."

The second gentleman looked to see but said nothing. Liga took the initiative to make introductions.

"Hello. My name is Liga and this is my friend Meladie."

The first gentleman returned with, "Hi. I am Oliver and this is my twin brother Orlando. Welcome to the entrance to the "Maze of Life." He extended his hand to shake, first to Meladie and then to Liga.

Meladie, who was very quick to see the significances of behaviors, thought him very solicitous and patronizing. He reminded her of the politicians she saw on TV when they were campaigning. The second gentleman stood somewhat behind the first and said nothing.

Welcome to the "Maze of Life."

Meladie deliberately extended her hand to him and said, "Hello, Orlando."

He shook her hand reluctantly and said nothing. Bluntly, Meladie asked Oliver, "Does Orlando not speak?" She was not one to beat about the bush.

Liga gave her a grimace and scolded, "Meladie!!"

"I'm just asking," insisted Meladie.

At which time Oliver interjected, "Oh, that's quite alright. You see, he only speaks to me, and he does so telepathically so I can say what he wants me to say. I'm really the one who doesn't speak."

"I don't understand," said Meladie inquiringly.

"Well, you see, Orlando is the the twin who has all of the ideas which I express for him. I, on the other hand, say whatever he wishes to express. It works well for both of us."

"The question is," said Meladie, "have you no thoughts of your own?"

"Of course not. I have no need of them. You see, I am well provided for by simply expressing Orlando's thoughts," replied Oliver.

"It seems to me that you cannot be a very sincere person if you do not speak for yourself," said Meladie. "How is anyone to get to know who you really are?"

"Well that is exactly the point. If people get to know who I really am, then they may judge me accordingly," said Oliver. "I can only gain the approval of others if I make them believe that I support their ideas whether I really do or not."

"Pardon my saying so, but that appears to be very dishonest to me," replied Meladie, as she turned away to end what she thought was a silly conversation.

After a few embarrassing moments of silence, Liga turned to Orlando to ask about getting through the maze. "You will help us, yes, to get through the maze to other side?"

Oliver answered, "Why of course. We do have an excellent plan, you see. Soon, Kate, the shrew mouse will return here for her supper of fine cheeses, which we provide. Each day she goes out to explore ways to get through the maze. That rope that you see is tied to her so that she can find her way back here. Kate will find the way for us. Mice are very good at mazes, you know."

"Excuse me!" chimed in Meladie. "You expect a shrew mouse to show us the way through the maze?" Looking at Orlando, she added, "Aren't you going about this the wrong way?"

"What do you mean 'The wrong way'?" asked Oliver for Orlando.

"The question is, 'Haven't you placed the cheese at the wrong end of the maze?'" asked Meladie with a rapidly growing impatience. "The shrew mouse will only get through the maze to get the cheese at the other end!"

"Hmm. You do have a point." said Oliver, speaking for Orlando. "But you see, if we could put the cheese at the other end, there would no need for us to have the shrew mouse find the other end for us because we would already be there. Now what do you say to that?"

"How long have you been using this plan?" asked Meladie.

"Why it has been forty-two days so far. But Kate told us just last evening that it will only be a few more days before she finds the other end." stated Oliver, speaking for Orlando.

"Has she ever said that to you before last evening?" asked Kate.

"Why yes." answered Oliver speaking for Orlando. "She has said it forty-one evenings in a row."

"Ugh!!" Meladie shouted at the top of her lungs. "This is so frustrating! She is never going to find it if you keep giving her cheese right here. Don't you realize how stupid that is?"

Orlando's eyes grew wide with shock, for he had never before witnessed anyone venting such frustration.

Oliver then turned to Orlando and very matter-of-factly asked him, "Are we too stupid to realize that?" Then his eyes grew wide as he said, "Oh, I don't think I should say that."

Yet again Liga interrupted. "Meladie, come aside. I must speak with you." She took Meladie by the arm and drew her away from the other two. "Meladie," She whispered, "We will get nowhere if you let your impatience get the better of you. Now you must show that you have the discipline. Good discipline makes patience a virtue."

"I know you are right, Liga, but it is just so frustrating to deal with them. They don't know what they are doing."

"This may be true, " whispered Liga. "But show a kind heart and perhaps come up with a better plan to suggest to them. It is only then that some good will come of it all."

Meladie was resolved to do as Liga suggested. Her advice made good sense. "I shall do as you say, Liga, I trust your advice."

CHAPTER 5

The Taming of the Shrew Mouse

It was just about time for Kate the shrew mouse to return for supper, and no sooner had Oliver opened a new package of cheese, Kate emerged from the maze entrance.

"Ah, right on time!" announced Oliver, almost as though he were speaking for himself. "Come and meet our new friends. This is Liga," he said, extending his hand in her direction. "And this is Meladie," pointing to Meladie.

"Hello," the two girls said in chorus.

Liga added, "We are so pleased to meet you."

"Hello," returned Kate rather timidly. Shrew mice are often very shy when they are introduced to new friends. She glanced over to the cheese which seemed to be beckoning her to the supper table.

Making the best of the situation as having been advised by Liga, Meladie attempted some friendly conversation with Kate. "Orlando, or Oliver, I'm not sure which one, has told us that you will find the way through the maze for us."

Kate hesitated, again glancing at the cheese on the supper table. "Why yes, I shall soon find the way," she said.

"When do you think that will be?" asked Meladie.

"In just a couple of days. Perhaps even tomorrow," she offered.

"Oh that would be wonderful if you could do it tomorrow. We could all be on our way," said Meladie, as if she were holding the shrew mouse to a commitment.

Oliver then said, speaking for Orlando, "Well, now that we've all met, let's sit down to supper. Then we'll let Kate get a good night's rest so she can set out early in the morning to continue her search through the maze. Her work day starts at 8 AM."

Kate immediately scrambled up the chair and leapt onto the table where her favorite cheese awaited her. The others took their places in the chairs on either side, with Meladie and Liga sitting on one side while Oliver and Orlando sat on the other opposite them.

They continued with small talk as they supped. Shrew mice you see are very small so whatever they say may be considered small talk. Each time Meladie brought up the subject of getting through the maze, Oliver, speaking for Orlando, changed the subject. Each time, Kate breathed a sigh of relief so she did not have to discuss her progress with the maze.

"What time will you be leaving tomorrow? At 8 AM?" Meladie asked Kate. "Perhaps I can go with you to help find the way."

Kate began to fidget and gave the others a worried look. "Oh, that's not a good idea," she suggested. "We shrew mice like to travel very fast when going through mazes. You would only slow me down. Besides, I leave much too early in the morning."

Meladie became very suspicious of Kate's answer. Why would Kate not want her help? Though Kate was a shrew mouse, Meladie, to coin a phrase, "smelled a rat." She made up her mind to follow Kate so she could see for herself exactly what was going on.

They all retired for the evening to get a good night's rest for the next day.

When morning came, Meladie awakened at 7:45 AM so she could accompany Kate. However, Oliver, speaking for Orlando, explained that Kate had left at 7 AM to get an even better start on finding her way through the maze.

"She is so conscientious about her work," he added.

Meladie suspected otherwise, for she was very suspicious that her suspicions were suspiciously correct.

"Well perhaps I can follow her path by using the rope about her waist to see if I can help. I'll start out immediately," insisted Meladie.

She took up the rope that was almost completely extended, and entered the maze to determine just how far Kate had progressed. When Meladie turned the first corner, there she saw the rope coiled in one huge pile. "She cannot be very far away," thought Meladie. As she turned the second corner, she found that her very suspicious suspicions were correct. There slept Kate with her daily allotment of lunch cheeses, as yet untouched.

"Kate! Wake up!" she shouted.

Not only did she wake, but she instinctively leapt to her feet as shrew mice do when startled.

"What do you think you are doing?" asked Meladie accusingly.

"Oh, dear. Oh, dear," she whined. "I'm afraid you have found me out. You see, I have not been searching for the way to the end of the maze."

"And why have you not?" Meladie asked.

"Oh please don't tell the others. But you see, there is no reason for me to find the way, for I have everything I want right here at this end."

"Oh, Kate," judged Meladie, "How dishonest you are to use Oliver and Orlando in this way."

"But I don't mean to. It's just that they give me everything I need right here. I have no incentive to go elsewhere. I know there is no cheese at the other end. If there were I should be able to smell it and find it," protested Kate.

"But have you no pride, you naughty little shrew mouse?" scolded Meladie. "You have been taking their cheese without doing any work for it."

"I know," said Kate. "But isn't that what mice do?"

"Well it's not what they should do," said Meladie. "Not only is it dishonest, but it is stealing. You are betraying your friends by lying about your helping them, when, in fact, you are doing nothing for them at all. You are a deceitful little shrew!"

"But have you no pride,
you naughty little shrew mouse?"

"I don't suppose you would consider keeping this our little secret?" Kate asked timidly.

"Absolutely not!" stated Meladie in about as firm a voice as she had. "How could you even suggest such a thing? Have you no conscience at all?"

"Well there is no harm in trying," stated Kate.

"Yes there is in this case. And trying to make me a part of your lowly scheme! I'll have none of it," stated Meladie very emphatically. "Now you are coming with me to confess to the others what you have been doing all this time for forty-two days."

Poor Kate knew she was trapped and had to face the music, so to speak.

CHAPTER 6

The Comedy of Errors

When morning came, it was Kate who was first up and ready to lead the others to Center Maze Estate where the Dowager Countess Malaprop lived. Kate was a little nervous about leading the others, for not only did she assume that responsibility, but she also had to regain the confidence of the others that she could be a good and helpful friend.

One by one the others arose ready for their new adventure. First there was Liga dressed and ready to be off. It was her hope that if Kate could find her way to the Center Maze Estate, then perhaps she could also lead Liga to Latvia soon after. After all, they did have cheese in Latvia, even if imported. She gave Kate a bright and cheerful "Good morning," which Kate anxiously returned.

Next up was Orlando who said nothing to the others. It was not his wont to speak to anyone until Oliver was there to speak his thoughts. Both Liga and Kate offered him a "Good morning" anyway, to which he simply nodded. Oliver did follow close behind, however, and spoke a "Good morning; good morning" for them both.

Finally, but not too long after, Meladie appeared. As you may know by now, she was not always at her best first thing in the morning, but she did get out her "Good mornings" to everyone and was obviously not to be held back on ceremony; she was ready for the day's journey. Her single-mindedness of purpose forced her to add, "Are we all ready? Let's get started."

"But wait!" said Oliver, speaking for Orlando. "Kate hasn't yet had her breakfast cheese."

"Oh, no thank you," said Kate.

The others were astonished by this. Each and every one stood there with mouth agape, for never had Kate ever refused a piece of cheese of any kind, let alone breakfast cheese, which just happened to be her favorite.

"Why won't you have some cheese this morning?" asked Liga.

"Yes, you've never before turned down your breakfast cheese," stated Oliver, speaking for Orlando. "Besides, you will need your strength to get us through the maze."

Even Meladie was surprised at Kate's refusal.

But Kate stood firm, showing great willpower. "Well, you see," said Kate, "I have not yet earned it, and I no longer wish to accept your charity for doing nothing."

Meladie knew that Kate was resolved to stand on her newly acquired value system so she offered the following suggestion. "Why don't we take some cheese with us so Kate can have some later. That way she will have a chance to earn it by leading us through the maze!"

All thought that a good idea, but perhaps Meladie spoke without fully realizing the consequences of her suggestion. But the five of them started out on their journey with great enthusiasm and anticipation of good fortune.

There were many decisions that had to be made, for each time they came to a juncture, Kate had to decide which way to turn. She would stop and sniff, hoping to pick up the scent of the Dowager Countess's stale and musty cheese. At times she would turn to the right. Other times she would turn to the left. The others followed quietly, not wishing to disturb Kate's concentration. All felt confident that Kate knew how to proceed.

After several hours of turns and twists along the patterned paths of the maze, The group came upon what appeared to be the exit to the maze.

"Kate, you did it!" they all shouted. "You found the exit."

Could it be possible that they had come upon the exit so soon and without passing through the Dowager Countess's Center Maze Estate?

Kate, however, looked distraught, and their celebration was short-lived. They realized almost simultaneously that the exit was not an exit at all, but the very entrance where they had begun. All of Kate's twists and turns had simply been a comedy of errors. Kate had led them back to where they started.

"Kate, you did it!" they all shouted. "You found the exit."

"Oh, this is just too hard!" complained Kate. "I can't do it. I have lost the ability to pick up the scent of the Dowager's cheese. I'll never get you there as I had hoped."

It was at this point in time that Meladie realized that her earlier suggestion to bring along some cheese as an incentive for Kate had been counter-productive. Kate could not pick up the scent of the Dowager's stale and musty cheese because the scent of the fresh breakfast cheese they had brought along only served as a distraction for poor Kate. So the very cheese that had brought her to Oliver and Orlando in the first place had only served to bring her back again. What were they to do?

CHAPTER 7

Measure for Measure

Meladie was astute enough to realize exactly what the problem was. She suggested, "I think we should give Kate another chance. The problem with the first attempt was simply not her fault. It was our fault. In our attempt to be nice to Kate by bringing along her breakfast cheese for later, we obscured the scent of the cheese at the Center Maze Estate. I therefore suggest that we leave that cheese behind so Kate can more fully appreciate the scent she means to pick up. Kate? Would you be willing to try again without our bringing any cheese for you?"

"Oh, yes!" she said enthusiastically. "But we must do more than just leave the cheese behind. As much as it breaks my heart to say it, we must bury the cheese right here so there is no scent of it in the air."

The others were all astounded by Kate's self-sacrificing proposal. If they had not been convinced before of her reformation, they certainly were convinced now. Imagine Kate suggesting that they bury her cheese! No one could have anticipated such a sacrifice.

So all were resolved that Kate should have a second chance. Oliver was given the task of burying the cheese before they left, and they set out once again.

"Liga was losing her balance."

This time, Kate measured every step carefully. At each intersection, she would stop and sniff dutifully, and make a decisive choice about which way to go. To the others she seemed much less hesitant about her progress than she had exhibited on the first try. She instilled confidence in the others which was lacking on their first attempt. Kate proved to the others that she was a professional cheese sniffer with abilities the others could not match.

On one occasion she stopped and sniffed, then turned to the others and simply smiled without saying a word. It was a smile of confidence which reassured the others that Kate was on the right track. With carefully measured steps she moved on. And measure for measure they all followed her without hesitation.

Soon they reached a juncture where Kate, for the first time, stopped and seemed somewhat perplexed about which way to go. She turned to the others to share her thoughts.

"We need to make a decision about which one of two ways to go," she declared. "If we go to the left, we can take the safer route which winds down through the gorge and back up again. It is a difficult walk and will add about four hours to our destination, but I'm confident we can all do it without incurring any injuries."

She then presented them with the dilemma. "If we go to the right, we will save the four hours time, but at great risk, for we must then cross over the gorge on a narrow tree that had fallen across the deepest part of the canyon. It will require good balance and sure-footedness."

After some hesitation, Kate added, "I need you to tell me which way you wish to go."

Meladie was the first to speak up. (Of course she was.) "I would like to take the short cut to the right and cross over the gorge rather than take four hours of hiking down the gorge and then up again."

Orlando disagreed so Oliver said, "That's easy for you to say, for you are young and agile; but we are not in such good shape and somewhat overweight. If we were to fall, we could be seriously injured."

"What about you, Liga?" asked Kate. Liga hesitated, then offered, "I stay with Meladie, but I am afraid to look down from high place.

"I will help you get across, Liga," offered Meladie. "We can do it together."

"Okay," said Liga. "I will try if you stay close with me."

And so Kate had her plan. She would send Meladie and Liga to the right, while she would escort Oliver and Orlando to the left.

"Meladie and Liga," she said, "you can find your way from here to the Center Maze Estate very easily. Take the path to the right, which will lead you to the tree bridge over the gorge. Once you cross the bridge, you need only to remain on the pathway which will take you to your destination not very far away. I will lead Oliver and Orlando to the left and through the gorge. Hopefully, we will meet you later at Center Maze."

Now the word 'hopefully' sounded more like a prayer than a certainty to Meladie, but then again there really are no 'certainties' in life. Unless, of course, you count the love and support of one's family.

But the thought of family and being away from them made Meladie somewhat forlorn for a spell; especially as she and Liga watched Kate and Oliver and Orlando move toward the path which would take them through the gorge. They moved away slowly with a measured pace. And measure for measure they were soon out of sight.

Her attention, however, quickly turned to the task at hand as she said to Liga, "C'mon. Let's get started toward the tree bridge." And they turned to their affairs.

It was not long after that they could see the approach to the gorge crossing, and as they drew closer, they could also see that there might be some difficulty involved, for the tree which lay across the chasm was quite narrow and of course had no railing of any sort to hold on to.

Liga began to pale as they approached the thin rail of a tree which certainly could be no wider than a gymnastic balance beam.

"Oh my God!" Liga gasped. "I cannot do this. I be sure to fall. I should have gone on with others."

Now Meladie, also with some trepidation herself, knew that she must put on a brave demeanor for Liga. "You can do this, Liga. Just think of it as though you are walking on the balance beam in gymnastics class. It's really not any more difficult than that!" stated Meladie reassuringly.

Meladie was not sure she had offered her the right example of encouragement when Liga confessed, "But you see I also fall off balance beam sometimes. But not so far down."

Meladie advised, "Just stick close to me and don't look down. Hold my hand and we'll be across quickly."

Liga was somewhat embarrassed that she was not as brave as Meladie considering that she was at least seven years older. She had no choice but to take Meladie's hand and follow.

Meladie placed one foot on the beam and steadied herself. She then added the other foot and began to move forward. Without looking down, Liga followed, grasping tightly to Meladie's hand.

They moved across with short measured steps being careful not to lose their balance. Neither of them looked down but kept focused on the other side straight ahead. Measure for measure they kept making progress. As they approached the other side, Meladie was about to step off the beam onto firm ground, when she sensed that Liga was losing her balance. Meladie quickly leaped forward, and with all of her might, yanked Liga forward to safety.

What seemed to them both as an eternity was really not very long at all. As a matter of fact, they reached the other side in less than ten minutes. As they stepped onto solid ground, both simultaneously let out a screech of joy that could be heard for miles. Not that they were aware of anyone else being within miles. But Meladie could not help but wonder if Kate and the others might not have heard their shouts of celebration echoing through the canyon.

And just so, the most difficult part of their journey was complete. As soon as they composed themselves, Liga offered her thanks.

"Thank you, Meladie. You save Liga's life. You see, I look down at last second and lose balance. Thank you for saving Liga."

Not knowing how to respond, Meladie simply sighed deeply and smiled at Liga. "You're welcome," she said. "We did it together."

Meladie knew she had a friend forever.

CHAPTER 8

Much Ado About Nothing

With the palace in sight, Meladie and Liga raced through the remaining meadow anxious to meet the Dowager Countess Malaprop. But as they approached, they could see another hurdle set before them. The palace was surrounded by a moat designed to keep out strangers and enemies. Not that the Countess knew of any enemies who might do her harm, but one could never take too many precautions to prevent bad things from happening, especially in an area so remote from most of civilization. You see, the palace was even farther away from civilization than Alpena, Michigan.

Now that is pretty far.

Nonetheless, the two girls had to deal with this newly confronted obstacle which the moat provided. There was a drawbridge, but that could only be opened from the inside by the Dowager's guards.

Liga thought perhaps they could get someone's attention inside by shouting out their desire to enter. "Hello! Is anyone home?" she called out.

"Can you lower the drawbridge?" Meladie added at the top of her voice.

After about five minutes of shouting, they remained quiet to see if there were any response whatsoever. But there was not.

Next Liga suggested that they just swim across the moat. After all, it was not very wide.

"Can you swim, Meladie?" she asked.

"Why yes, of course I can swim, but I don't think that's a very good idea," said Meladie pointing to something on the other side.

"I don't think that's a very good idea."

Liga got the point immediately when she noticed what Meladie was pointing toward. On the opposite bank lay two sizable creatures which served as the palace's first line of defense. They must have been at least twelve feet long with heads that measured fourteen inches across.

Now Meladie did not fear many things, but she suspected that crocodiles of this size could swallow her in one quick gulp. She quickly calculated the odds of a successful swim under these circumstances and concluded that such a risk was not worth taking.

Liga agreed without argument.

So what were they to do? They weighed several options:

1. They could continue screaming out until someone heard them and decided to let them in.
2. They could walk around the moat until they came to a place where there was another crossing.
3. They could just sit and wait until the others arrived and their little shrew mouse Kate would know how to get them in.

In the first instance, they decided that all the screaming and yelling would only cause them to lose their voices. Since it had not worked before, they were sure this option simply would not work. (option 1: eliminated.)

Option two was briefly considered, but eliminated because of the vastness of the property. As they looked to the left, the castle wall appeared to extend almost as far as the eye could see. As they looked to the right, the wall extended at least as far as the other direction. No, this option could take them days, and there was no guarantee that they would find another crossing. Since they were both exhausted from the travel they had already accomplished, they decided not to consider the journey around the moat. (option 2: eliminated.)

And so they were left with just option three. They were resigned to sit and wait for the others. There really was no doubt they they would decide on option three, for they both were very tired and welcomed the chance to just sit for a while and do nothing.

But they sat there just for a brief period, just minutes when something began to happen. Although they were not sleeping, they were both in a restful state with their eyes closed when they heard a loud clanking noise which brought them both to a startled awakening. As they sprang to their feet and looked to see what the din was, they saw that the drawbridge was being lowered. Once in place for them to cross, out marched two lines of soldiers in formation with full battle gear consisting of helmet, shield, and lance. The soldiers stopped on the bridge in two straight lines and stood at attention.

At first the two girls thought them to be a welcoming ceremony, but they seemed too serious to be simply ceremonial. The girls stood there and watched in awe as the soldiers remained motionless at attention. Their brightly colored uniforms of red and black seemed to glow in the sunlight. No one spoke for several minutes as the soldiers just stood silently at attention.

But soon there emerged two more uniformed men who walked through the middle of the two lines of soldiers to the end of the bridge where they stopped to address the girls, who waited patiently to see what was to follow. The taller of the two men was obviously the one in charge, for he wore many ribbons and medals on his chest and a sword at his side. The other, not quite as tall, seemed to be his aide, for he carried a roll of documents which he handed to the taller man.

The taller unfurled the documents and spoke. "Good morning." There was a slight pause as the aide whispered something to the taller man, who then continued, "Sergeant Dumdrivel informs me that it is now past noon, so I stand corrected and must begin again."

After some shuffling of feet, he began again. "Good afternoon. I am Captain Captain, Captain of the Royal Guard."

Once again the Sergeant interrupted with whispered instructions.

The Captain began again. "I am General Captain, Captain of the Royal Guard."

More whispering.

"Err, I am Captain General, General of the Royal Guard."

More whispering.

"Err, I am Captain General, Captain of the Royal Guard."

No more whispering.

By this time Meladie was becoming very impatient, but Liga, anticipating Meladie's reaction to the Captain, quickly put her hand over Meladie's mouth and gave her an admonishing look.

The Captain went on, "Sergeant Dumdrivel will now give you the orders of the day." He handed back the unfurled documents to the Sergeant.

"On behalf of Captain General, Captain of the Royal Guard, I do hereby order the arrest of both of you for spying on the Royal Palace."

Liga immediately jumped up to say, "No, you cannot do that! We are not spies. We have just come to visit Dowager Countess Malaprop."

More whispering between the Captain and the Sergeant.

The Sergeant went on, "I do hereby absolve you of the charge of spying, but place you under arrest for trespassing. You did not give proper notice to the Countess of your arrival."

At this time Meladie spoke. "Oh but that is what we are here for now, to give notice to the Countess that we are here to visit. So please tell her we are here."

More whispering between the Captain and the Sergeant.

The Sergeant proclaimed, "You are hereby absolved of the crime of trespassing. I therefore welcome you to the Royal Palace of the Dowager Countess Malaprop. And now Captain General, Captain of the Royal Guard, will escort you to the Palace."

"Much ado about nothing!" moaned Meladie very quietly to Liga as the girls fell into formation with the guards and followed the Captain across the bridge leading into the palace grounds.

CHAPTER 9

All's Well ... (So Far!)

As Meladie and Liga marched over the bridge and through the castle door, they caught their first glimpse of the inside. They were simply awed by the huge open expanse of beauty before them. There were rows and rows upon rows of garden paths leading through the most extensive flower gardens anyone could ever have imagined. Each section was patterned with its own colors. They passed through the bright red on one side and the bright yellow on the other. Ahead there were purples and whites and greens and blues. And off in the distance, beyond the orange and maroon, they could see the palace. It stood majestically before their eyes.

Meladie turned to Liga and whispered, "It looks like the castle in Disney World, but its so much larger."

"I have not been to Disney World, but this is truly amazing," Liga responded.

At this time Sgt. Dumdrivel ordered in a loud booming voice. "There shall be no talking in the ranks while marching!"

Liga quickly placed her hand over Meladie's mouth for she feared Meladie would have a contrary remark for the Sergeant.

They soon approached the palace where, just out front among the orange tiger lilies, there stood a tall woman dressed in gardening clothing that was somewhat soiled from her work. She wore long gloves and a huge bonnet that protected her from the sun. The trowel she held appeared to be of gold which reflected the sun's rays brightly.

She stopped her work as they approached and were ordered to a halt before her by Sgt. Dumdrivel, at which time Captain General saluted and announced, "I bring before you guests of the palace." The soldiers did an about face and left the two girls standing before the woman doing the gardening.

Meladie thought it unusual that the gardener would be the one to greet them, but she thought perhaps they were short of staff since there was no one else to be seen.

"Are you the gardener?" she asked. "You do such beautiful work."

The woman simply raised her eyebrows as she looked down at the two girls.

Liga was mortified by Meladie's comment. She did have a little more awareness of class protocol and knew that the woman was not a gardener. She politely knelt before the woman hoping that it would be enough to silence Meladie.

Meladie got the idea and knelt before woman as well. She was embarrassed at her mistake. "Well how was I to know!" she whispered to Liga without turning her head. From this point on she thought it would be better just to follow Liga's lead.

"are you the gardener?" Meladie asks Duchess Malaprop, much to Liga's embarrassment.

The woman spoke. "Good afternoon. No, I am not the gardener. I am Countess Malaprop. Welcome to the Palace at Center Maze. Now please get up. It is not necessary for you to kneel before me when we are not in the palace court. And even there, a simple curtsey will do."

The two girls stood and were happy to know that the Countess was friendly and informal.

"Now please tell me, who are you two and why did you come?" asked the Countess Malaprop.

"I am Liga from Latvia and this is my good friend Meladie."

"I come from Michigan," said Meladie somewhat nervously. She realized immediately that she spoke too loudly and too fast. It was very unusual for Meladie to feel ill at ease in anyone's company, but so many things were unusual since she left home.

"And what brings you here?" the Countess asked.

Both girls began answering her question at the same time so the Countess did not understand a word.

"My, my!" she interrupted, raising a hand to quiet them. "Perhaps it might be better if just one of you conversated at any given time. Please serenity yourselves. There is no need for you to be nerveless here."

The two glanced at each other before Liga took the initiative. "Well, you see, Madam Countess, we are trying to reach the East gate to determine our destinies."

Meladie, waiting her turn to speak, added, "Yes, and we were told that we have to pass through Center Maze to do it."

"And whom intelligenced you this?"

Meladie volunteered the answer, "Well, you see, it was one of your past workers, Kate. the shrew mouse."

"Oh yes. My little friend Kate. I do miss her so. She was so very industrial. I've had to take care of my flower beds myself since she deployed. She was such a large assistance."

As the Countess Malaprop spoke, Meladie thought what an unusual way to speak. But she said nothing for fear of being impolite.

"Well then you may be happy to know that she is on way back," announced Liga. "She is so afraid that you be angry with her."

"Oh no!" said the Countess. "I was so desired that she would retrospect."

Meladie wasn't sure she understood, but she got the gist of what the Countess was saying and added, "Kate should be here later this afternoon. She had to take the others the long way to make it easier for them. You see, there are two others with her."

"Oh wonder bar!" exclaimed the Countess.

"Please tell me, Countess Malaprop, what is this beautiful white flower you are working with right now?" asked Meladie.

"Why that, my Dear, is called a day lily, for it is only in bloom for one full day. You are so lucky to have come today to see it at its fullest beauty," explained the Countess.

"Something as beautiful as that should live forever," proclaimed Liga.

"Yes, isn't it a shame that it only blooms for a day," added Meladie.

"Oh, no, my Dear. You see it is because of its short life that that we can appreciate it so much more," explained the Countess.

> ... A lily of a day
> Is fairer far in May,
> Although it fall and die that night -
> It was the plant and flower of light.
> In small proportions we just beauties see,
> And in small measures life may perfect be.[4]

"But come now," said the Countess. "You will all be deflated to know that the King arrives with his revenue tonight to supper with us. You may all join us. Our good King The Third Richard III visitates us once each year to see how his subjects feel about his kingdomain. This night he brings the Crown Prince with him."

"Oh what fun!" said Meladie.

"But we have no clothes to change. We cannot meet King and Prince like this," protested Liga.

Now had it been just the King coming, Liga most likely would not have said what she did, but the word 'Prince' did peak her interest.

"This is not a problematic," said the Countess. " The royal tailor will be here soon. I'm sure he can take care of your wardrobial requirementations. You can all stay the night if you wish, and be on your wayward in the morning."

"Oh thank you so much, Countess Malaprop. You are so kind," said Meladie.

"Yes. Thank you, added Liga.

"Now come in and we'll begin preparationaries for tonight," instructed the Countess.

CHAPTER 10

The Third Richard III

Meladie and Liga were shown to their rooms by one of the maidservants assigned to attend to their preparations for dinner with the Third King Richard III, along with his royal following. The girls were given a room with two full-sized beds and a connecting bath. The mattresses were high off the floor, so much so that a foot stool had to be used to step onto the bed. Each bed was topped with matching canopies. The carpeting was of the finest Moroccan silk and the antique furniture reminiscent of Louis XVI of France. The girls were overwhelmed by the room's splendor. It was the most magnificent bedroom either of them had ever before seen.

As the maidservant began preparing their bath, the two of them unrestrainedly leapt upon their beds and began bouncing on the large soft mattresses until they brushed their heads on the canopies above. What fun!!

When they got down from the beds and began to contain themselves, Liga looked out the palace window upon the courtyard below.

"Meladie, come here. Quick! Look!"

The girls watched as Captain General, Sgt. Dumwit, and the royal guard were escorting Oliver and Orlando to the palace. But there was no sign of Kate. What could possibly have happened to her?

It was right at that moment that the maidservant announced that the royal tailor awaited them in the dressing room. They would have to find out later what happened to Kate.

Meladie and Liga... "leapt upon their beds and began bouncing."

As they entered what was called the dressing room, they were introduced to the royal tailor, who just happened to be their old acquaintance, Mr. Skylark.

"You know the drill," he said. "Meladie, step up and we will have you pick out your evening gown first. Then we'll do Liga's."

"How did you get to be the royal tailor?" asked Meladie.

"Each year the dowager Countess Malaprop invites me to practice my skills for the King's feast. The King has been very pleased with my work so he has appointed me thus."

The three of them chatted while the gowns were being selected, and Mr. Skylark told them about some of the previous celebrations and some of the magnificent gowns the women wore. Meladie picked a beautiful gown that was royal blue, her second favorite color. It was a perfect fit, and she thanked Mr. Skylark wholeheartedly. Liga's gown was of white satin with gold trim and a tiara to match.

"Oh, Liga," exclaimed Meladie. "You are so beautiful. You look like a fairytale princess."

Mr. Skylark admitted it was his best work ever.

At that moment, the Countess entered. "My, my! How beautiful you both look. Soon you will meet the Third King Richard III. In 30 minutes we will have introductions and hers devers in the artist room. We shall then propose to the dining room for the King's feast. Now don't be tardisome. Ta ta!" She left just as quickly as she had come in.

"How exciting!" said Liga. "I have never see a King before."

"Nor have I," said Meladie, affectedly. Her tone was playfully imitating the Countess's manner of speaking. "And I have never before seen 'her devers.'" Returning to her normal voice, she added, "What are her devers anyway?"

Mr. Skylark volunteered the translation. "She really means hors d'oeuvres. And what she calls the artist room is really the drawing room. It has nothing whatsoever to do with art."

"Why doesn't she say what she means?" asked Meladie.

"Well," said Mr. Skylark. "She just can't help herself. So you must be polite and not correct her."

"You mean she make mistake?" asked Liga.

"Most often," was the reply. "But one can usually get the drift of what she means to say."

"The question is," said Meladie, "should one take such liberties with words and what they mean?"

"Trust me," warned Skylark. "Just go with it. Not even the King is disposed to correct her. And remember, proper protocol requires you not to speak to the King unless he addresses you first. Now go and have a wonderful time.!"

The girls did have a wonderful time. The dowager Countess Malaprop very graciously introduced everyone to the Third King Richard III. No one seemed to mind that the Countess used so many words incorrectly. The King then announced that the young Crown Prince, who had just turned 18, was attending this affair for the first time, and the King hoped all would make him feel welcome as all stood about and chatted pleasant conversation.

Meladie noticed that the Prince was staring at Liga, who blushed each time her eyes met his.

It was not long before the Prince approached the two girls and began conversing, mainly with Liga. Soon Meladie grew tired of just listening to the two of them, who seemed to have forgotten that she was standing right next to them. She quietly slipped away and moved closer to where the King was standing. He was very observant in noticing the social dynamics of the drawing room, and he began a conversation with Meladie, who was so pleased that she now had the opportunity to converse with the King.

"Why are you called the Third King Richard III? Shouldn't you be Richard V?" asked Meladie. The room grew very quiet, for no one had ever before had the brazenness to ask this question of the King.

But the King quickly diffused the tensions of the moment by smiling at Meladie. He immediately had taken a liking to her, for never before had anyone so young been so unafraid in his presence.

"Well you see, my Dear," he began. "My father, the great Second King Richard III was not very good at numbers, and he thought that it would help all who lived in the Kingdom if they didn't have to count too high. It was his hope that no one would ever have to count beyond the number three. So instead of his becoming Richard IV, he chose to become the Second King Richard III, which of course, in keeping with the newly established tradition set by my father, made me the Third King Richard III."

"Oh, I wish he hadn't done that. It just seems to make everything so confusing," said Meladie. "And what are you King of?" asked Meladie. "Do you, like other Kings, have a Kingdom?"

"Oh yes. One is not really a King if he has no kingdom. My kingdom extends far to the North and even farther to the South. It is called Himmel-land."

Meladie had never before heard of any place called Himmel-land.

"You will most likely come there one day. I am sure it is a part of your destiny," said the King.

At that precise moment the chimes were struck and the announcement "Dinner is served" was made, and all were led to the dining room. The elongated dining table was centered beneath a most beautiful crystal chandelier. The tables settings were of gold. Meladie noticed that each setting had a name plate designating where each guest was to sit. Before all were told to sit, She also noticed some whispering between the Prince and the King, and then more whispering between the King and the Countess, who then gave instructions to one of her serving staff. Meladie's name plate, which had been next to Liga's at the far end of the table, was then switched with with the Prince's, which had been next to the King. Since the Prince had started the whispering, Meladie did not have to wonder why the switch had been made, but she was pleased to be placed next to the King.

After dinner, all were called to the ball room, where the Prince and Liga danced most of the evening while the others joined in. It was a magical evening of splendor.

CHAPTER 11

A Winter's Tale

When Meladie and Liga returned to their room, there was Puck the owl waiting for them on the sill just outside their palace window. They ran quickly to open it so they could tell Puck what a good time they had, but he had a very stern look on his face.

"I don't mean to spoil yoour evening, but I come to remind you of your almost blunted purpose, which is to find what destiny there is in store for each of you. You must now get back on task," instructed Puck with solemnity.

"What must we do next?" asked Meladie.

"First you must get a good night's rest. Then you must seek the 'Carousel of Destinies' where your journey will be completed," explained Puck.

"I dó not understand," said Liga. "What is 'carousel'?"

"Is it like the merry-go-round at Disney World?" asked Meladie.

"Indeed, That is a carousel," said Puck. "But this is a carousel of the gates of destiny. There Lady Fortune will select the gate that is right for you, and you will be on your way to the destiny that has been selected for you. It will be the destiny for which you are best suited based on your special abilities and character," explained Puck.

You must seek the "Carousel of Destinies."

"But where is the Carousel of Destinies?" asked Meladie.

"You must seek it 'East of the sun and West of the Moon,'"[5] directed Puck. "Therefore, yoou must begin at dawn, or yoour destiny may never be reached."

"Is that near Latvia?" asked Liga with a worried look.

"No, my Dear," said Puck. "But if Latvia is your destiny the carousel will get yoou there."

"Will it take me back home?" asked Meladie.

"It will take yoou home and beyond," answered Puck.

"Oh, I would so like to get home soon," pleaded Meladie. "How do we get there?"

"Arise at dawn while the palace guards are still asleep at the East gate. There, Oliver and Orlando will be waiting for yoou with Kate, who will lead yoou through the back half of the Maze of Life. I have placed her favorite breakfast cheese at the exit so she can find her way."

"Will the Carousel of Destinies be there,?" asked Meladie anxiously.

"Oh no," said Puck. "That is just the beginning of your days' journey. Here, you are in summer. You must pass through fall and winter in order to reach spring where the Lady Fortune will be waiting for yoou."

"But that will take months!" protested Meladie.

"No," reassured Puck. "Yoou see, summer, fall, winter, and spring are simply areas that you must pass throooough. If yoou remain on task, yoou will reach your Destiny early the next day. Once Kate gets yoou throooough the Maze and into Fall, yoou will pass the 'bare ruined choirs where late the sweet birds sang.'[6]

Then on to Winter where yoou must go

> '... between the wood and frozen lake
> the darkest evening of the year.'[7]

It is then that you will reach Spring where you can rest from yoour long night's journey and just romp about. Then follow the morning sun and yoou will reach Lady Fortune and the Carousel of Destinies."

"But it sounds so complicated," protested Meladie. "What if we get lost?"

"Trust in yoour abilities and yoou'll not fail," reassured Puck. "Remember, I shall be watching."

It was at this point that he left the girls to their own devices. Although they thought the directions he gave were rather vague, they agreed it best to try to follow as best they could beginning with a good night's rest, but, in truth, neither of them was very well rested when the time came to leave just before dawn. The truth of the matter is that neither of them had slept a wink of the owl's eye.

Needless to say, they were a bit bleary eyed when they met the others. As they reached the east gate to exit Center Maze, they were perhaps a few minutes late, but as the owl predicted, they found the guards still asleep and Kate, Orlando and Oliver waiting.

Kate immediately took over leading the others with a newly found confidence.

"C'mon!" she ordered. "we must get going." Not only was she a confident leader, but a very capable one as well. As the others followed closely, Kate sniffed and turned and maneuvered them through the maze, for, you see, the "incentive" was properly placed so she could lead all toward their destinies.

When they reached the east exit, the better part of the day lay ahead. And yes, Kate was well rewarded with the succulent breakfast cheese which Puck left for her. The others praised her work, as well as her willingness to share her meal, for they had reached Fall as promised.

It was a lovely Fall day when they arrived. The sun was shining brightly and the air was crisp. The tall pines swayed with the breeze, and the leaves of the live oaks were turning yellow. As they followed a pathway leading them deeper into Fall, the wind picked up and the leaves began to fall. The choirs of birds became silent as they left to fly South. As they got deep into the fall, they could feel the temperature dropping, and they knew Winter was not far off.

Before long, they reached a divide. Yes, the proverbial fork in the road would force them to make a choice of which way to go. How could they possibly know which was the right path to take? While there was discussion and disagreement, there was no resolution. Kate suggested the left, and Oliver said Orlando preferred the right. Meladie agreed with Kate, but surprisingly enough, Liga sided with Orlando. Oliver could not be the tie-breaker, for he had no thoughts of his own.

It seemed to all that perhaps Puck had let them down with his instructions until Meladie remembered what he had said. She now realized that what seemed vague to her before, now had significance.

Just a short way down the path to the right, she could see what Puck meant. She pointed to the large oaks. "Look!" she exclaimed. "The limbs of those large oaks are bare. The birds are all gone. That's what Puck meant by 'bare ruined choirs where late the sweet birds sang.' We must take the right pathway to Winter."

The decision was made, for just as Kate had solved the Maze, just so Meladie had figured out the word puzzle given them by Puck. All agreed to follow Meladie down the right path.

As they progressed through late Fall, they could all feel the temperature dropping. The sky became gray and darkened to a charcoal soon to be black. They knew Winter could not be far off. More and more, the once yellow leaves were rust colored on the cold ground. Yes, they were in winter now, and surely it was to be their winter of discontent, for all became frost, and then ice. Meladie guessed to herself that the faren-celsius must be about 15 degrees.

They soon arrived at the frozen lake where their path came to an abrupt end, right smack in the middle of the lake's shore. Another decision had to be made. Their first thought was to walk directly across the lake, the shortest route through Winter, But what if the ice did not hold fast beneath them? It was now so dark that they would not be able to see any treacherous cracks which might cause them to fall through into the freezing water beneath the surface. Surely they would all drown if that should happen. They would have to circumnavigate the lake, but which way should they set out? To the right there were dark woods, and to the left there were snowy fields. Either way would be difficult.

Once again it was Meladie who remembered Puck's directions. "We must go to the right," she directed. "Puck said 'Between the wood and frozen lake the darkest evening of the year.'"

"Yes," added Liga. "I remember too he say that."

And so, between the woods and frozen lake it was, as once again they huddled together and moved as one. Oliver, Orlando, and Liga took turns at the front to block the wind for the others much as the Antarctic penguins did to get through those severe wind storms at the bottom of the globe. There was no point in Meladie or Kate taking the lead; they were simply too small to block much of the wind.

As they passed between the woods and the frozen lake, the black sky began to get lighter and lighter in small degrees at first, and they could feel the temperature rising as well. Spring could not be far away. Meladie once again estimated the faren-celsius to be approximately 55 degrees, which she this time shared with the others as encouragement to press on.

By early dawn, with the red sun rising, all were relieved to know that it was Spring. The song of the first morning lark broke the silence, and soon the choir of birds sang once again. Flower buds were bursting with color, and once again Spring's rebirth arrived.

CHAPTER 12

All's Well That Ends Well

It was just a short walk to the Eastern shore where they were to meet Lady Fortune, who would send each of them to his or her destiny. They circled round and jumped for joy that their journey was complete. They took a few moments to romp:

> O dance along the silver sand,
> And beat the turtle drum,
> That youth may last forever
> And sorrow never come. [8]

Little did they know that their journey was just beginning, for there stood Lady Fortune next to the Carousel of Destinies. She called them forth one by one to enter the carousel to be whisked off toward their own personal destiny forever.

First, there was Oliver. As he was called to step up to the carousel boarding platform, Lady Fortune pulled the lever to spin the huge wheel bringing Oliver's gate of destiny before him. In large white letters, the gate's label read as follows:

POLITICIANS AND ALL OTHERS WHO HAVE
NO THOUGHTS OF THEIR OWN

The gate opened and Oliver stepped forth to hear the metal clank shut behind him. The wheel spun again and Oliver was sent to his destiny.

Next up to the boarding platform was Orlando. His gate came to a screeching halt before him. It's label read as follows:

PHILOSOPHERS AND ALL OTHERS WHO THINK BUT DON'T DO.

He too boarded and was swept away.

Kate was next. She nervously awaited the gate chosen for her. Once again the carousel stopped. Kate's gate had just a single word:

CHEESE

"That's for me!" she shouted and boarded happily.

Then came Liga. As she stepped up to the boarding platform, Meladie sadly wondered if they would ever see each other again. They had become such good friends.

LATVIA AND SO MUCH MORE!

Liga smiled to know that she would be returning home but paused to look back at Meladie. Neither said a word but for both it was a difficult parting. Of course they would see each other again, but that happy reunion would not take place for several years to come.

As Meladie stepped up to the boarding platform, the last in line, it was Puck who made a perfect landing on the post beside her. He had come to offer her his support in the completion of his duties to watch over her.

Meladie's future read as follows:

FIRST HOME
THEN ANYWHERE AND EVERYWHERE

She turned to Puck and said, "I'm so happy to be going home again, but what does this mean?"

"It means, my Dear Meladie, that yoou have special abilities and talents that may take yoou anywhere yoou wish to go and do anything yoou wish to do; but yoou must chooose wisely. To realize yoour dreams, yoou must practice due diligence in your studies and steadfastness in your character. Only then will many gates be open to you. Look through your gate now and you will see what future gates will be open."

Meladie looked through her gate far into the future. She saw architecture and science; the arts and theater; medicine and astronomy; music and dance; athletics and mathematics and so much more. The number of gates was endless.

"Remember," Puck emphasized, "Diligence in study and steadfastness in character. Then yoou will be free to chooose."

With Puck's advice in mind, Meladie was ready to board the carousel of destinies. But not before turning to Puck. "Thank you, Puck, for all you have done and for watching over me. I shall be forever grateful."

She passed through her gate for home and her future. As the carousel spun her away, she felt a strange sensation. Her body seemed weightless as she spun slowly upward with her eyes closed. She soon became drowsy and lost consciousness. It was not long (at least so it seemed to her) that she gradually regained her feeling. She knew she was lying comfortably in her bed with her eyes shut. And when she forced her eyes open, she knew that she was home. And then came the "revelation." She sprang up to a sitting position with both arms raised and shouted,

"I KNOW WHAT I WANT TO BE!!!"

"I Know what I want to be..!"

CHAPTER 13

Epilogue

Kate the shrew mouse moved to Holland and went into the cheese business. Her "EAT-EM" cheese became world famous. She was later invited to the King's Feast at the Center-Maze Palace, thereby becoming the first mouse to ever sit at a dinner table with a King.

Oliver was elected to the U.S. Senate where he became a master of the filibuster. His success depended on his not having any thoughts of his own.

Orlando moved to Greece and wrote several books on philosophy.

The Athenians erected a life-sized statue honoring him. It still stands next to those of Plato and Socrates.

Mr. Skylark moved back to Venice where he continued his vocation as a merchant. He married a young lawyer named Portia.

Liga did make it back to Latvia, but when she turned 20, the young Prince asked for her hand in marriage. They had a daughter who later became the first female to rule Himmel-land as Queen.

And then there is Meladie. It would be pointless to reveal her destiny at this time because she was still so young at the end of our story. In truth, she would have been a success no matter what she chose because she remained diligent in her studies and steadfast in her character. Suffice it to say, she realized her destiny and made the world a better place.

Puck the owl was very proud of her.

ENDNOTES

[1] Title "Like the melody …" from the Robert Burns poem "My Luv Is Like the Red Red Rose."

[2] page 8 - "We are such stuff …" from Shakespeare's The Tempest, Act IV, scene i.

[3] page 17 - "O wad some power …" from the Robert Burns poem "To a Louse."

[4] page 48 - " …a lily of a day …" from the Ben Jonson poem "It Is Not Growing Like a Tree."

[5] page 57 - "East of the sun …" from a Norwegian Folk Tale.

[6] page 57 - … bare, ruined choirs …" from Shakespeare's sonnet LXXIII.

[7] page 57 - " …between the wood and frozen lake …" from Robert Frost's poem "Stopping By Woods."

[8] page 61 - "O dance along …" from the poem by Ian Serrailier.

Printed in the United States
By Bookmasters